AUDREY WOOD **THE**
NAPPING
Illustrated by
DON WOOD **HOUSE**

HARCOURT, INC.
San Diego   New York   London

Requests for permission to make copies of any part of the work
should be mailed to the following address: Permissions Department,
Harcourt, Inc., 6277 Sea Harbor Drive, Orlando, Florida 32887-6777.

Library of Congress Cataloging-in-Publication Data
Wood, Audrey.
The napping house.
Summary: In this cumulative tale, a wakeful flea atop a number
of sleeping creatures causes a commotion, with just one bite.
[1. Sleep — Fiction. 2. Fleas — Fiction.] I. Wood, Don,
1945— ill. II. Title.
PZ7.W846Na 1984   [E]   83-13035
ISBN 0-15-256708-9
ISBN 0-15-204689-5 pb

KK JJ II HH GG FF EE DD CC

The original paintings were done in oil on pressed board.
The text is Clearface Roman, set by Thompson Type,
    San Diego, California.
The display type is Clearface Bold, set by Thompson Type,
    San Diego, California.
Separations by Heinz Weber, Inc., Los Angeles, California
Printed and bound by Tien Wah Press, Singapore
Designed by Dalia Hartman

Printed in Singapore

For Maegerine Thompson Brewer

There is a house,
a napping house,
where everyone is sleeping.

And in that house
there is a bed,
a cozy bed
in a napping house,
where everyone is sleeping.

And on that bed
there is a granny,
a snoring granny
on a cozy bed
in a napping house,
where everyone is sleeping.

And on that granny
there is a child,
a dreaming child
on a snoring granny
on a cozy bed
in a napping house,
where everyone is sleeping.

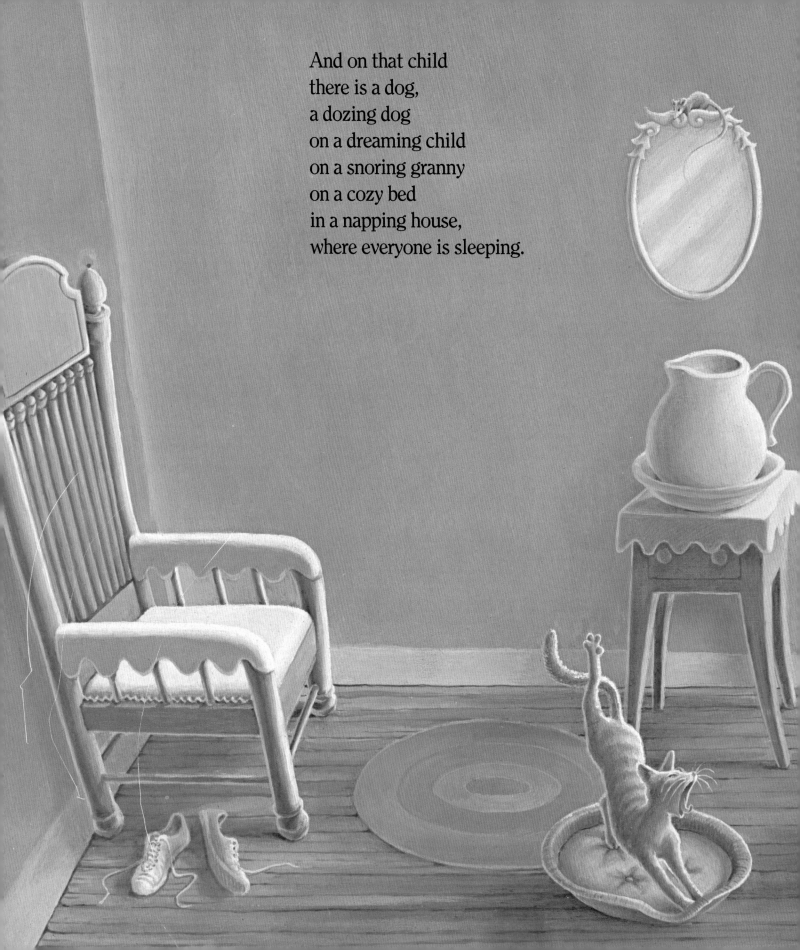

And on that child
there is a dog,
a dozing dog
on a dreaming child
on a snoring granny
on a cozy bed
in a napping house,
where everyone is sleeping.

And on that dog
there is a cat,
a snoozing cat
on a dozing dog
on a dreaming child
on a snoring granny
on a cozy bed
in a napping house,
where everyone is sleeping.

And on that cat
there is a mouse,
a slumbering mouse
on a snoozing cat
on a dozing dog
on a dreaming child
on a snoring granny
on a cozy bed
in a napping house,
where everyone is sleeping.

And on that mouse
there is a flea. . . .

Can it be?
A wakeful flea
on a slumbering mouse
on a snoozing cat
on a dozing dog
on a dreaming child
on a snoring granny
on a cozy bed
in a napping house,
where everyone is sleeping.

A wakeful flea
who bites the mouse,

who scares the cat,

who claws the dog,

who thumps the child,

who bumps the granny,

who breaks the bed,

in the napping house,
where no one now is sleeping.